Amateur Writings from a lost soul

Whispers of Love, Echoes of Loss

A Journey by Shalini

Table of Contents

Acknowledgement

Hi, My Dearest Pattu,

You are the reason I found the strength to write this—our story, our love, and everything we shared. You gave me the love I had always longed for, a love so pure and unconditional. You gave me moments that I will cherish for the rest of my life, and even in your absence, you have left me with a void that speaks to the depth of our bond.

In your memory, I am writing this, my dear Nila, because you are and will always be my heart, my inspiration, and the light that guides my words.

With all my love,
Amma

Author's Note

This book is born from both love and loss, from memories and the aching space left behind by my daughter, Nila. She was my moon— my Nila. Her name, meaning "moon" in Tamil, suited her perfectly, for she was the light in my life, the source of my quiet strength and boundless joy. She was only with us for a short time, but her presence was profound, filling every corner of our lives with love.

One day, Nila was diagnosed with Primary Amoebic Meningoencephalitis (PAM), a rare and relentless illness caused by a microscopic amoeba. PAM is unforgiving; it takes hold swiftly, and despite all medical efforts, it claimed my precious Nila in a way we were powerless to prevent. In a matter of days, my world shifted from warmth and laughter to an emptiness I had never known.

Writing this book has been my way of honoring Nila's memory, of remembering the joy she brought to my life, even as I navigate a world without her. These pages are filled with letters, poems, and reflections from a mother to her child, sharing the thoughts and moments that now live on only in memory. They capture my conversations with her, the moments of laughter, of love, of longing, and the journey through grief that has forever changed me.

As you read, you may notice that I speak to her as though she were still here. In a way, she is. Her spirit, her light, her love—they remain with me, guiding me each day. This book is a way to share that light with you, to let her warmth touch others, and to offer a glimpse into the powerful bond between a mother and her child. I hope that through these words, you will come to know the beauty of Nila's short life and understand the enduring love that will always remain.

Introduction

I am beginning to write these words in what feels like the darkest chapter of my life. There's a heaviness in my heart, a fog of emotions clouding my mind, and yet, here I am, putting pen to paper. I can't say for sure if these words will resonate with anyone, if someone else might feel the same sorrow, or if there is even anyone out there going through a similar situation. But if there is, I hope these words reach you and remind you that you're not alone.

I am not a writer, nor do I pretend to be one. I am not a wise sage who has uncovered the secrets of peace and happiness. I'm just a regular girl from a city, a face in the crowd, trying to make sense of a life that often feels unfair. I'm neither a philosopher nor a scholar; I'm just someone who has seen enough to know that life doesn't come with a guidebook. There are no guaranteed answers or magic formulas – just day-by-day attempts to understand and, hopefully, find some peace.

People ask, "Why write? Why now?" I don't have a perfect answer. All I know is that writing gives me a release – a way to pour out the thoughts that weigh me down. I hope, just maybe, that these words will reach someone who feels a similar weight. I hope they find comfort, or even just the reassurance that they aren't carrying their burdens alone.

This book isn't filled with expert advice or the "secrets" of successful living. I'm not someone who has reached extraordinary heights or conquered life's biggest challenges with ease. I didn't grow up surrounded by abundance or privilege. As a first-generation graduate from a middle-class family, I grew up with one goal: to make my family's life a little easier, to give back to the parents who sacrificed so much for me. But that journey hasn't been easy, and success isn't as clear-cut as it sometimes appears. Success, for me, isn't about wealth or status; it's about survival, responsibility, and a quiet hope for peace.

In a world that seems obsessed with "winning," I often feel like an outsider. I don't fit the mold of what society defines as success – I'm not the CEO of a major company, I don't have a fairytale love story, nor a picture-perfect life. And I know I'm not alone in this. There are so many of us, just trying to make it through, trying to find meaning in the everyday grind of life.

I've read countless stories of people who've "made it," but there are fewer stories about people who, like me, are just trying to make do. When you come from a family that has struggled, where basic needs like food, shelter, and medical care aren't always guaranteed, your idea of "success" shifts. Life isn't about grand accomplishments – it's about the smaller victories, the moments when you manage to ease your family's burdens, even just a little.

Throughout this journey, there have been times when I've longed for someone to understand, to share the weight of my responsibilities. Yet, as I've learned, understanding doesn't always come easily. Sometimes, people around you don't realize the load you're carrying, or they take your strength for granted. But if you're reading this, and you've felt that same longing, know that you're not alone. There's a silent strength in those of us who carry on, even when no one else sees our struggles.

This book is my attempt to make sense of my own life, and maybe, in doing so, to offer a bit of solace to others. I am here not just as myself, but as a representative of the quiet resilience of middle-class individuals everywhere, especially those who feel unseen and unheard. This is my story, a mother's journey of receiving a love I had yearned for since childhood – a love given by my child, now beyond reach. In sharing this, I hope to create a sanctuary for those whose lives have veered from the expected path. To you, dear reader, I say: your story is precious. May you find solace and kinship in these pages, knowing that even amid life's unforeseen sorrows, your experiences are deeply meaningful.

As we embark on this journey together, I want you to know that this book isn't about reaching some final answer. It's about the journey itself – the ups, the downs, the messiness of it all. And maybe, just maybe, in my words, you'll find a reflection of your own story, and a reminder that you're not alone.

Whispers of You: The Beginning of Nila

> *"From the very first breath, you became the heartbeat of my existence."*

The Moment of Revelation

August 15, 2023 – 8:30 a.m.

In the quiet solitude of the early morning, life spoke to me in the softest, most delicate whisper. As the world lay still, I found myself holding a small, unassuming piece of plastic, yet within its fragile frame, two faint lines bloomed, carrying the weight of a revelation. I gazed at those lines, barely breathing, as the realization unfolded within me—gentle at first, like the dawn's first light, and then, all at once, as a wave of pure, uncontainable joy. It was as if a secret had been spoken just for me, a sacred message woven directly into my heart.

Clutching the test, I felt a tremor rise within me, a kind of wonder I'd never known. I crossed the room in a daze, my footsteps light, almost reverent, as though each step was part of a journey unfolding toward a new world. I found Vijay, my voice catching in my throat, eyes wide, and breath caught as I held up that small, miraculous sign. "We're going to be parents," I whispered, each word wrapped in awe, the sound so fragile, it barely left my lips. Yet the words, though soft, reverberated through every corner of my heart, and in that instant, I felt life shift beneath my feet.

In that moment, the entire world blurred into silence and light. The misunderstandings that had once crept into the spaces between us faded, slipping away like shadows at dawn. You, our tiny miracle, our secret yet to be known, bridged the distance between us, knitting together hearts that had, at times, felt worlds apart. In that single, precious heartbeat, I became more than I had ever been—a mother, a keeper of a love so fierce and pure, it redefined my soul. It was as if, for the first time, I was seeing the world in its truest form, awash in color and light, all because of you.

In the days that followed, I carried that moment close, feeling the steady warmth of this new love settle deep within me. The promise of you, so delicate and yet so profound, wrapped itself around me, and with each passing day, I felt myself grow. You, my love, were the beginning of everything—a tiny spark that illuminated every corner of my heart, a quiet revolution that turned my life into something sacred and beautiful.

A Heart Awakened

As the days slipped by, I felt myself transformed in ways I had never anticipated—not only in body, as I nurtured the fragile life growing within, but in spirit, as a profound sense of purpose began to root itself in my soul. No longer was there the restless drift of days gone by, where life felt like a puzzle missing pieces. You were my anchor, the gentle thread weaving together each fragment of my existence, creating a tapestry of love and promise. All those quiet moments of longing, the whispered prayers in the stillness, the questions I had carried—they all seemed to converge in you, their answer taking shape within me.

I began to dream of a life that would unfold with you at its heart. I saw glimpses of a world filled with your laughter, of moments spent cradling your tiny hands as you took your first steps, of days spent guiding you, watching as you discovered the world with wonder in your eyes. Each dream stitched itself into the fabric of my heart, wrapping around me like a warmth I had never known.

In the quiet hours, when the world had settled into its own soft rhythm, I would sit with my hand resting over my belly, speaking to you as if my words could reach across the barrier of flesh and time. I whispered to you of love—the kind of love that endures, that would forever hold you safe, even if unseen. I told you stories of family, of the hands and hearts that waited eagerly for your arrival, ready to surround you with a lifetime of joy and comfort. I spoke of the world you would soon enter, of the wonders that awaited your curious gaze, of the sunrises and flowers and the songs of birds that I longed for you to experience.

In these moments, I felt a closeness, a bond that transcended everything I had ever known. I wanted you to understand that from the very beginning, you were cherished, loved in a way so complete and unwavering that even my words felt inadequate. Each whisper carried a promise—a promise that I would be there for you in every way, that I would nurture and protect you, that I would give you all the love I had ever dreamed of receiving. You, my precious child, had transformed me, filling my heart with a purpose as deep and boundless as the ocean.

And so, as I waited for you, I spoke to you in these hushed, sacred moments. I let my heart pour out every dream, every hope, as if each one was a gift I could give to you before you even arrived. You were, and always would be, my cherished one, my heart's answer, my Nila.

The First Flutter

As the weeks drifted by, you became more than a quiet presence within me. You were no longer just a whisper, a dream taking shape; you were a vibrant, living part of me, sharing every breath, every heartbeat. It began with the faintest flickers, delicate as the brush of butterfly wings against the walls of my womb—a tender rhythm, a language known only to you and me. Each flutter and soft kick carried a message, a silent communication that wrapped around my heart like a gentle embrace. Every tiny movement was a reminder of the miraculous soul growing within me, each sensation drawing me closer to you, deepening a love I hadn't known was possible.

In those sacred moments, when the world outside felt distant and muted, I would place my hand over my belly, hoping to capture every precious movement, every sign of you reaching out to me. The gentleness of your presence, the dance of life within, felt like a gift—one that I held with reverence. You were speaking to me, in your own way, letting me know you were there, listening and feeling. These moments became my universe, a secret world where only you and I existed, bound together by a love that was both ancient and new.

Your Appa would sing to you, his voice filling the room, casting melodies into the air that I imagined wrapping around you like a warm, protective blanket. Each song was a lullaby, a gentle introduction to the love that awaited you. One day, as his voice drifted through the quiet, I felt a sudden, tender kick—a response, a gentle nudge that took my breath away. It was as if you were dancing along with his tune, reaching out to let me know you felt our presence, that you were part of our shared world. My heart soared with joy, and in that instant, I felt a bond so profound that words felt too small to contain it.

That kick was more than just a movement; it was a promise—a signal that you were not only listening but reaching out, connecting with us from within. It was a conversation without words, a pledge of love, and a declaration of your existence. In that precious moment, I knew we were woven together, inseparable, connected in a way that nothing in this world could ever break. You, my dearest one, were already my world, filling my heart and soul with a love that would remain with me forever.

The First Glimpse of You

Then came the day I saw you for the first time, your tiny form captured in shades of black and white on the ultrasound screen. There, within those blurred shadows, you appeared—tiny hands curled gently, fingers like delicate petals, little legs that seemed poised to dance, and those eyes that, though closed, seemed to contain the vastness of the universe within them. I stared, utterly mesmerized, as if the world had stilled for this single, sacred moment. My heart swelled, filling with a love so overwhelming it brought tears to my eyes. You were my dream come to life, my miracle made real, and in that fleeting instant, I wanted to cling to your image, to hold it close as if it could last forever.

The screen's grainy, monochromatic glow felt like a window into another realm—a place where time paused, where you and I existed in our own world, untouched by anything outside. Every scan felt like receiving a love letter from you, a whispered message that spoke directly to my soul. I would gaze at the shifting images, tracing the outlines of your tiny body, letting each flicker, each heartbeat, carve itself into my heart. Each glimpse of you left me breathless, a reminder of the life growing within, a life that had become the very center of my being.

I remember the sound of your heartbeat, a steady, rhythmic echo that resonated deep within me. It was a song only I could hear—a melody that was both ancient and new, binding us together in a way words could never capture. And in those moments, I found myself talking to Ammachi, sharing the miracle of you with her, letting her know about this extraordinary love that had blossomed in my heart. I told her about the promises I was already making to you, promises to protect you, to cherish you, to fill your life with every ounce of love I possessed.

Yet, as I held those black-and-white images, so precious and fleeting, I couldn't help but long to see you in color—to witness the vibrant beauty of your eyes, the softness of your skin, the light of life that I knew would shine from within you. I dreamed of the day I would finally see you, not as a shadowy image on a screen, but in all the hues of life, warm and real in my arms. Though you were not yet born, you had already claimed every inch of my heart, painting my world in shades of love and anticipation that I had never known before.

Those grainy photographs became my treasures, pieces of you that I carried with me, symbols of the connection we shared even before you entered this world. And with each passing day, my longing grew— to see you, to hold you, to let you fill my life with the color and warmth only you could bring. You, my dearest one, were already my heart's truest song, echoing through every corner of my soul.

The Promise of Family

As you grew within me, so too did the love that surrounded you—a love that blossomed like a garden in full bloom, tenderly nurtured by every member of our family. You were the heartbeat of our home, the gentle soul whom everyone adored even before they saw your face. Your Appa, Ammachi, Thattha, Avva, Thattha, your chithi, chithapa, and mama—each of them fell under the spell of your presence in their own beautiful way, drawn together by the quiet magic you had already brought into our lives.

Your Thatthas would arrive with small treasures, delicate gifts wrapped with love, as if each one was a whisper of their devotion. Tiny toys, soft blankets, and thoughtful trinkets filled our home, turning each room into a sanctuary of anticipation and warmth. These gifts weren't merely objects: they were wishes, blessings, and promises—a silent vow that you would be surrounded by people who loved you fiercely, people who would hold you close and keep you safe in this world.

As each day passed, your presence became a quiet, unifying joy that touched every corner of our lives. Every flutter and gentle kick you made was celebrated as if it were a miracle, a sign of the life we all awaited so eagerly. You, my love, were our shared dream, the little miracle who had drawn us all into a collective embrace of hope and wonder. We would gather together, each with a heart brimming with affection, imagining the softness of your tiny hands, the sparkle in your eyes, the beauty you would bring to this world.

In the warmth of those gatherings, we would sit and dream together, our thoughts woven with laughter and love. We painted pictures with our words, imagining the little expressions you might make, the curious gaze you would cast upon the world, the laughter that would fill our home when you arrived. And in those moments, you became more real to us, more beloved than anything we had ever known.

We held you in our hearts long before we could hold you in our arms. Every conversation, every gentle laugh shared in anticipation of you was a testament to the love that awaited you. You were not simply an awaited arrival; you were the essence of our family, the piece that completed us, the child who would know only love from the very start. With each passing day, our collective dream of you grew richer, deeper, like a tapestry woven from the softest threads of affection.

And as we waited, our hearts whispered promises into the quiet—promises that you would always be cherished, that your life would be filled with warmth and love, that you would be held close by a family whose devotion to you was boundless. You, my precious one, were already the soul of our home, the thread that bound us all, and our lives became infinitely more beautiful in anticipation of the day we would finally meet you.

The Journey to Meet You

April 5th dawned softly, the air thick with a sense of quiet anticipation. There was a gentle nudge within me, a feeling so delicate yet unmistakable—a mother's intuition, an unspoken whisper that today would be the day you entered our world. As the morning light filtered through the curtains, a thrill rippled through my heart, a combination of excitement and the faintest tremor of fear. I felt a shift within, a stirring that grew stronger with each passing moment. And then, by 9 a.m., the sign I had been waiting for arrived. My water broke, and with it, a wave of emotions surged through me, filling me with a love so profound it brought tears to my eyes.

"Vijay!" I called, my voice trembling as I tried to contain the torrent of feelings within me. He rushed to my side, his face a mixture of joy and concern, and together, we embraced the reality of what was unfolding. We were about to meet you, our cherished miracle, the one we had loved even before you took your first breath. Every second felt like an eternity as we made our way to the hospital, our hands clasped tightly, hearts racing in unison.

Upon arrival, the bustling hospital faded into the background as I lay waiting, surrounded by the steady hum of medical instruments. The room was filled with a quiet tension, a hush that seemed to settle over everything. Nurses and doctors moved with purpose, their voices low as they monitored your heartbeat. I closed my eyes, feeling the weight of the silence—a silence that felt too heavy, pressing down on my heart. And then, a moment of hesitation. A nurse looked at me, her gaze soft but tinged with worry, and she asked gently, "Is there anything that usually elicits a response from the baby?"

My mind raced back to our little secret, a simple word that had become our shared joke, a familiar sound you seemed to recognize. With a soft smile, I whispered, "Biryani." In that instant, as if you understood, your heartbeat returned, strong and vibrant, echoing through the room like the sound of hope itself. The tension broke, replaced by a wave of relief that washed over everyone, but especially me. You, my love, knew how to reassure us, how to fill our hearts with joy even before we met you face to face.

That heartbeat was more than just a sound; it was your presence, your spirit, a promise that you were there, ready to meet us. Even in that moment, you had a way of making us laugh, of bringing lightness into a room shadowed by worry. You were already showing us the strength and love that would define you, reaching out to us from within, letting us know that everything would be alright.

As I waited for the next phase to unfold, I held that moment close, savoring it like the sweetest of gifts. You were not only my child; you were my courage, my joy, my little miracle, filling my heart with a love deeper than I had ever known. With every beat of your tiny heart, you gave me strength, and with every breath, I felt our connection grow stronger. You were about to enter this world, but already, you had filled my life with an unbreakable bond that would live within me forever.

The First Cry

And then, finally, I heard you—a sound so pure and powerful that it shattered the silence, filling the room and my heart with a joy beyond words. Your first cries broke through the air, a melody of life and love that I had longed to hear. Amid the blur of voices and gentle reassurances, I heard the doctor say, "It's a girl." In that moment, my heart soared, lifting me to a place beyond happiness, a place where dreams become real. I had wished for a daughter, a little angel to fill my life with grace and wonder, and here you were, my wish granted, my miracle come to life. Even in my half-conscious state, a wave of relief washed over me, followed by a surge of love so profound it took my breath away. Every part of me was drawn to you, an overwhelming need to hold you, to feel your warmth and know you were real.

When they placed you in my arms, it was as if the world around us faded into soft focus, leaving only you and me in a cocoon of quiet awe. I looked down at you, and there it was—the gaze I had dreamed of, the look I had imagined countless times. Your eyes, wide and full of wonder, found mine, and in that single, silent connection, I felt a love so vast it seemed to expand beyond the boundaries of my heart. You looked at me as if I were your whole world, as if in my arms, you had found your first and final home.

In that sacred moment, I understood the purpose I had been seeking, a purpose that was as clear and certain as the beating of my heart. You were so small, so incredibly perfect, each delicate detail a masterpiece. Your tiny hands, curled softly around my finger, your warm breath against my skin—all of it felt like a miracle, a moment suspended in time that I wished I could capture forever.

As I looked into your eyes, I felt as if I were gazing into an entire universe—a boundless expanse of love, trust, and promise. There, within your innocent gaze, I saw a reflection of the purest love I had ever known, a love that had quietly waited its entire existence to meet you. In that instant, you gave me something words could never capture: a reason to be, a purpose that would fill my days, color my world, and shape the very fabric of my soul.

Holding you in my arms, I felt as if my entire life had been leading to this singular moment. Every breath, every heartbeat, every choice I had ever made seemed to converge here, in this quiet, extraordinary instant. I knew then that I was not merely holding my child—I was holding my reason, my heart, my world. You were everything, and in that gaze, you filled every corner of my soul with a love that was boundless and timeless, a love that would live in me for eternity.

Our Days Together

Every day with you was a gift, a symphony of small, sacred moments that I held close, like treasures wrapped in love. In the gentle rhythm of our days, I would read to you from a Tamil letter book, reciting each word softly, as if these letters held the secrets of the universe. Your tiny hands would reach for the pages, fingers curling around each one as though you longed to understand their meaning. You listened with an intensity that filled my heart with wonder, your eyes wide, absorbing every sound, every syllable. It was as if you understood each word I spoke, as if the language of love that connected us made every letter sing. Those quiet moments with you became my sanctuary, a space where the world faded away, leaving only you and me, bound together in a soft, unbreakable bond.

Our home, too, became a sanctuary of love, filled with the devotion of everyone who adored you. Your Vijay—your beloved Appa—would cradle you in his arms, his voice turning gentle and playful as he whispered stories of his dreams for you. I would watch as he held you close, his eyes soft with a tenderness that only you could bring out, his entire world reflected in your gaze. He would sing lullabies, his voice a soothing melody that seemed to wrap around you like a warm embrace, each note a promise that he would always be there for you. And when you smiled at him, he would beam, his laughter filling the room like sunlight breaking through the clouds.

Ammachi, your grandmother, held you as if you were the most fragile and precious of treasures. She would rock you back and forth, murmuring old songs and blessings, tracing your tiny hands with her own, marveling at the miracle of you. She would tell stories of our family's past, as if weaving you into the legacy of our ancestors, connecting you to a history rich with love and resilience. She would look into your eyes and see the future, a continuation of everything she had lived and loved, and in those moments, her heart was complete.

Your Thattha—your wise, loving grandfather—had a gentle way of reaching out to you, his eyes lighting up each time he saw you. He would sit beside you, talking in soft tones, sharing the wisdom he had gathered over a lifetime. He'd offer little gifts, small tokens he thought might catch your attention—a wooden rattle, a colorful charm—each one chosen with care, each one a silent prayer for your happiness. Every gift he gave was more than just a toy; it was a symbol of his love, his hope that you would always feel joy, that your life would be as rich and full as his love for you.

Avva, your other grandmother, brought warmth and sweetness wherever she went. She would place tiny flowers in your hair, singing to you in her melodious voice, a gentle lull that seemed to make you glow. She would sit beside you, sharing quiet moments that only the two of you could understand, her love flowing to you like a stream, pure and clear. She delighted in every expression you made, watching as you explored the world with wide-eyed wonder, her heart swelling with pride and joy with each new discovery.

Your other Thattha, ever playful, had a special way of drawing out your laughter. He would bounce you on his knee, making silly faces that would send you into fits of giggles, his deep, hearty laugh joining yours, a duet of joy that would echo through the house. He found delight in every little thing you did, seeing you as a light that brightened every corner of his life. With him, you shared a language of laughter, an unspoken connection that needed no words.

Your Mama, young and full of energy, became your playmate, the one who would dangle toys above your crib, his voice animated and joyful, filling the room with a light-hearted energy that you couldn't resist. He would make funny noises, dance around just to see you smile, his heart filling with a love he had never known, a devotion that took him by surprise. You became his little sidekick, his joy, the one who made every day brighter.

And Chithi, your loving aunt, would hold you close, marveling at your tiny hands, your soft cheeks, and the way your eyes followed her wherever she went. She would talk to you about all the dreams she had for you, her voice gentle and full of promise, as if she could already see the wonderful person you would become. She loved you fiercely, protective and nurturing, ready to give you every bit of love she held within her heart.

And even though he was far away, your Chithapa had his own special place in your life. He would call, filling the screen with his smile, singing songs just for you. You would start by looking at him with a tiny frown, as if you were disappointed he wasn't there beside you. But as his voice poured over you, that frown would melt away, replaced by the brightest smile, your little face glowing with joy. His love crossed every mile, every barrier, and his song became a lullaby that soothed and delighted you, a bond shared across the distance, connecting you both in a way only family can.

Chinna Ammachi, your other loving grandmother, was always by your side. She would cradle you day and night, as if letting you out of her sight was unthinkable. She watched over you with an almost fierce devotion, her eyes full of love and protection, as though we were too careless and only she could keep you safe. Her presence was a constant source of warmth, her love boundless, a watchful guardian who ensured that you felt cherished every moment. She loved you as deeply as the roots of a tree hold to the earth, steady and unwavering.

Your Priya Chithi, the youngest in our family, embraced her role as your aunt with all the warmth and devotion in her heart. Though she was the smallest in our home, she became your Chithi in the fullest sense, holding you close, marveling at every tiny gesture you made, her face alight with love. She would cradle you with all the tenderness and care of someone far beyond her years, her small hands full of big love. To her, you were the center of her world, and she poured all of herself into loving you.

And Periya Mama, ever doting, would call you "papa, papa" in his joyful voice. From afar, he would speak to you as if you were right there, sharing his love through the screen. He would tell you about all the plans he had, promising to buy you a little "nadavandi" when he returned, eager to spoil you with affection. His words, full of delight and tenderness, always made you giggle. You could feel his love even through the distance, as if each word he spoke reached out and wrapped you in a warm hug.

And then there was your Thattha, who adored you with all his heart, would sit beside you, his gaze full of tenderness and love. He would cradle you, humming softly, his voice gentle and comforting, his love evident in every glance, every smile. When the time came for him to leave, he found it harder than he had imagined. His eyes grew misty as he kissed your forehead one last time, his heart heavy with the sorrow of parting. Tears welled up as he said goodbye, his love lingering in the air, a promise that he would always carry you in his heart, even when he was far away.

Together, we all adored you. You had a way of making everyone around you smile, bringing laughter to each room you entered, filling our lives with a joy we had never known. And in those rare moments when someone shed a tear, you would look at them with your wide, knowing eyes, and then, as if you felt their sorrow as deeply as your own, you would start to cry too. It was as if you shared in the world's emotions, a little soul so sensitive and tender, already attuned to the beauty and fragility of life.

Every day with you was a celebration, a gentle unfolding of love and laughter, a gift that bound us all together in ways we could never have imagined. You, my dearest one, were the heart of our family, a precious angel who had united us all in a love that was as infinite and pure as the sky above.

A Love That Endures

Even now, as I look back on these moments, my heart swells and aches with the love that binds me to you, a love woven into every corner of my being. I remember the promises I made to you, whispered softly as I held you close. I promised to protect you, to cherish you, to be the warmth and strength you would need to grow. I vowed to keep you safe from the world, to shield you with every fiber of my being, to wrap you in a love so profound that it would be your comfort and your refuge.

Though life's journey has taken you from my arms, that promise remains unbroken, unyielding. It echoes within me, a steady rhythm that beats with each pulse of my heart. It is a vow etched into my soul, unchanging, a constant truth that no passage of time can erase. I feel your presence in every breath, in every quiet moment, as if you are still here, just a heartbeat away, woven into the fabric of my existence.

You are my Nila, my moon, my guiding light. Though I cannot hold you in my arms, I hold you in my soul, cherished and remembered in the quiet spaces, in every sunrise and in every whisper of the wind. I carry you with me through each day, feeling the softness of your memory brush against me, gentle yet powerful, a reminder of the boundless love that connects us. You are the light that colors my world, a brilliance that fills even the darkest moments with warmth and beauty.

And as I live each day, I keep my promise to love you forever. I will hold you close within me, guarding every memory, every precious moment we shared. Your love is a presence that lives within me, a part of me that will never fade. You gave me purpose, a reason to be, a love so deep it stretches beyond the limits of time. Because of you, I understand that true love endures, transcending all boundaries, unbreakable and eternal.

In my heart, you will always be there—my cherished child, my sweet Nila. I am eternally grateful for the gift of you, for the joy and meaning you brought into my life. And even as life carries on, you are my forever love, my moon, my constant, and my promise to you endures, woven into the fabric of my soul. I will love you, Nila, for all of my days, with a love as steady and unending as the stars that watch over us both.

Unwritten Tomorrows: Letters to Nila

*"These letters were written in the hope of a future
I dreamt of for us—a future filled with milestones,
laughter, and love. They are messages from the
time when you were here, capturing my hopes for
all the beautiful tomorrows we would share
together."*

14th July 2024

My Dearest Pattu,

Today marks a truly special milestone—you have crossed your 100th day in this world. It feels like just yesterday that I held you in my arms for the very first time, yet these past 100 days have been filled with immeasurable joy, love, and wonder. As your mom, my heart overflows with emotions, and I wanted to capture this moment in words so you can one day look back and know just how deeply you are cherished.

From the moment I knew you were growing inside me, my life changed forever. The anticipation of your arrival was filled with dreams and hopes for your future. I wondered about your smile, the sound of your laughter, and the sparkle in your eyes. When you finally arrived, you exceeded every expectation—more beautiful, more precious, and more perfect than I could have ever imagined.

These 100 days have been a whirlwind of learning and discovery for both of us. I have marveled at every tiny milestone, from your first smile to the way your little fingers curl around mine. Watching you sleep peacefully, I often find myself dreaming about the wonderful person you will become. Each day with you is a gift, and I am endlessly grateful for the joy you bring into my life.

You have taught me so much already. Patience, for those moments when you cry and I can't quite figure out why. Strength, for the sleepless nights and the worries that come with being a new mom. And most importantly, unconditional love—the kind that makes my heart swell with pride and happiness every time I look at you. You have given me a new purpose and filled my life with a happiness I never knew existed.

I love the way you look at the world with wide-eyed wonder, finding fascination in the simplest things. Your innocence and curiosity are a reminder of the beauty in life, and I promise to nurture that sense of wonder in you. The world is vast and beautiful, filled with endless adventures waiting to be discovered, and I will be right there to help you explore it.

As you grow, I promise to be there for you every step of the way. I will be your biggest cheerleader, celebrating your successes and comforting you through your struggles. I will teach you kindness, empathy, and the importance of being true to yourself. I will encourage you to dream big and believe that you can achieve anything you set your mind to. And most importantly, I will always love you, no matter what.

There will be challenges ahead, moments when life may seem difficult. But I want you to know that you are never alone. I will always be here for you, ready to offer a hug, a listening ear, or a shoulder to cry on. Your happiness and well-being are my top priorities, and I will do everything in my power to ensure you feel loved and supported every single day.

The bond we share is something incredibly special, and I cherish every moment we spend together. From our quiet mornings to our playful afternoons, every second with you is a treasured memory. I love the way you light up when you hear my voice, the way you snuggle into my arms, and the sweet sound of your laughter. You have filled my heart with a love beyond words, and I am so grateful to be your mom.

As you continue to grow and discover the world around you, I hope you always know how deeply you are loved. You are my sunshine, my little miracle, and my greatest joy. These past 100 days have been the most wonderful of my life, and I look forward to a lifetime of beautiful moments with you.

Always remember, you are loved—not just by me, but by everyone who has the privilege of knowing you. Your grandparents, aunts, uncles, and friends all adore you and are excited to watch you grow. You have brought so much happiness into our lives, and we are all incredibly grateful for you.

Thank you for being you, my sweet Pattu. Thank you for the smiles, the cuddles, and the countless moments of joy. Thank you for teaching me what it means to love unconditionally. I am so proud to be your **அம்மா**, and I will always be here for you, cheering you on and loving you with all my heart.

Happy 100th day, my Pattu. Here's to many more days of love, laughter, and cherished memories. You are my everything, and I love you more than words can say.

என்றும் உன்னை நேசிக்கும்,
உன் அம்மா,
ஷாலினி

The Day I Knew You Were Mine

15th August 2024
My Dearest Pattu,

Today holds a special place in my heart—it marks one year since I discovered the wonderful news of my pregnancy with you. As I sit down to write this, I am overwhelmed by a wave of mixed emotions, each one filled with love and deep reflection.

A year ago today, my life changed in the most extraordinary way. I remember that moment vividly—the mix of excitement, surprise, and even a bit of disbelief as I saw those two pink lines. It felt as if the world had paused for a brief second, allowing me to fully absorb the magnitude of what was happening. The joy I felt was immense, but so were the uncertainties and questions about the future. It was a time of profound emotional turbulence, yet, through it all, there was a thread of pure, unadulterated love that remained constant.

In those early days, I found myself grappling with a whirlwind of thoughts and feelings. The reality of becoming a mother was both exhilarating and daunting. I wondered how my life would change, how I would adapt to the new responsibilities that lay ahead. There were moments of doubt and fear, but they were always accompanied by a deep, unwavering hope and excitement for what was to come.

Every step of the way, I was filled with a sense of awe and wonder, knowing that you were growing inside me—a little person who would soon become the center of my universe. As the months went by, those initial uncertainties gave way to a growing bond between us. Feeling your tiny movements for the first time was a moment of indescribable joy. It was as though you were already communicating with me, reassuring me that everything would be alright. Each day brought new discoveries and new reasons to smile, and my heart swelled with pride and love as I thought about the incredible little person you were becoming.

Throughout this journey, I was surrounded by love and support from family and friends. Their encouragement and understanding were invaluable, helping me navigate the challenges and celebrate each milestone. I often thought about how much they would adore you, and how you would bring so much joy to their lives as well.

Reflecting on the past year, I am filled with gratitude for the incredible gift of having you in my life. The early days of your life have been filled with both challenges and triumphs, and through it all, my love for you has only grown stronger. The sleepless nights, the endless feedings, and the moments of worry have all been outweighed by the immense joy and fulfillment you bring to my life. Every smile, every laugh, and every tiny achievement of yours is a reminder of how blessed I am to be your mother.

There have been moments of sheer exhaustion and moments of doubt, but there has also been an abundance of love and joy that far surpasses any difficulties. You have taught me more about patience, resilience, and unconditional love than I could have ever imagined. Watching you grow and develop has been a source of immense pride and happiness, and I am constantly in awe of the person you are becoming.

As we celebrate this special day, I want you to know how deeply loved you are. Your presence has brought so much light and happiness into our lives, and I cherish every moment we spend together. You have a special place in my heart, and that love will only continue to grow as you continue to grow.

Looking ahead, I am excited about the future and all the adventures we will share. I look forward to witnessing the milestones you will reach, the dreams you will pursue, and the person you will become. I am committed to supporting you, loving you, and being there for you every step of the way.

Thank you for being such a wonderful gift in my life. You have filled my heart with a love that I never knew was possible, and I am so grateful for every moment we share. As we reflect on this special day, I want you to know that you are cherished beyond measure and loved more than words can ever express.

என்றும் உன்னை நேசிக்கும்,
உன் அம்மா,
ஷாலினி

As I wrote this letter, my heart was filled with dreams of a beautiful future—a future where every milestone was a moment shared, every adventure was a step together. Today, I share these words in a world where those dreams remain forever unwritten, their promise silenced by your absence.

Yet, while the future I imagined for us became void, the love that bloomed during those moments still fills every corner of my heart. The hopes I held for you are now a quiet echo, but they are echoes of a love so profound that time cannot erase it.

These words are not just memories of what could have been; they are the testament of a love that transcends even the most profound loss. Though our journey together was brief, my dear Nila, you will always be a part of me, in every breath, every thought, and every beat of my heart.

The Big Step: My Journey with Nila

"With each step, I learned that love could be as soft as a whisper yet strong enough to carry me."

Beyond Loss

There comes a time in life when you start to believe you're ready for anything. You think you've weathered enough storms, endured enough heartbreaks, and overcome enough challenges that nothing else could truly shake you. You tell yourself, "I am strong; I've survived so much already." But life, in its quiet unpredictability, has a way of showing us that we are never truly prepared.

One day, I sat alone and asked myself, "Is there anything left in this world that could break me?" I thought I had faced all the trials life could throw my way. I had known hardship, I had endured struggle, and I had come through each battle scarred but standing. I was convinced that nothing could hurt me more deeply than I'd already been hurt.

But life, with its boundless capacity for surprise, had something unimaginable in store for me—a loss so profound that it stripped away every layer of strength I thought I had built. This loss took from me not just a part of my life, but a part of my soul. Losing you, my precious Nila, was not something I could ever have prepared for. Nothing in this world could have readied me for the pain of being separated from you.

We face so many challenges in this world—financial struggles, the pressures of work, the demands of relationships, the weight of debt and duty. These things test us, yes, but they are things we learn to endure, to conquer, to survive. But the loss of someone you love, the loss of a life that is intertwined with your own, is different. It's a sorrow that doesn't fit neatly into any category; it's a wound that never fully heals.

Grief, I have come to understand, is not a phase to "get over" but a new way of being. It's a shadow that accompanies you, a part of your soul that has been reshaped. The world around me looks the same, but everything feels different. Basic acts like eating, sleeping, and moving through the day have become mountains that I must climb. This sorrow has seeped into every corner of my life, making even the simplest tasks feel insurmountable.

And in this darkness, I find myself struggling to hold on to hope. The light I once saw in the world feels dimmer, and yet, life insists that I keep going, that I live through the pain, breathe through the grief, and find a way to carry this loss with me. It's a journey I never chose, but it's one I must endure, if only to honor the love I hold for you, my dear Nila.

This book is my attempt to capture that journey—the journey of learning to live in a world without you, the journey of carrying you with me in spirit, even as I face each day without you by my side.

There are days when the weight of existence feels almost unbearable, and I find myself asking questions that echo into the emptiness: "Why?" Why must I keep going? What is the purpose behind my being here? What am I supposed to learn from all this pain, all these endless challenges? Sometimes, it feels as though life is holding secrets it refuses to share, leaving me alone with questions that only deepen in silence.

There are days when I realize I don't want to be strong. I don't want to be the "independent woman" that life has molded me into, or the person that others look to as a beacon of resilience. I never asked for that title. All I want is a life that is simple, untouched by tragedy—a life filled with the quiet warmth of the people I love. Is that too much to ask? The idea of strength, of independence, feels hollow when it's forged through loss and hardship.

To be called strong is to carry a burden that most can't understand. Strength, people say, is an admirable quality, something to be proud of. But what if I don't want to be strong? What if I simply want peace? Strength does not make the weight of grief lighter; it only means that I am expected to carry it alone. Sometimes I think, "Yes, I am strong, but that doesn't mean I can withstand it all." I wonder, "Why me?" Why has life chosen this path for me, when all I wanted was something ordinary and full of love?

In my darkest moments, I feel as if life is a pre-written script, and I am merely an actor following a role I didn't choose. I watch my life unfold, events moving beyond my control, and I sit helplessly, wondering if anything I do will ever truly matter. And if everything is already written, if every sorrow is predestined, then what is the purpose of my struggle? Why do I keep fighting, keep running, when it feels as though the finish line is just an illusion?

I am filled with questions—questions that have no simple answers. The emotions within me are deep, complex, and often beyond explanation. These are feelings that only someone who has walked through the same fire, who has faced a similar loss, could truly understand. I am searching, longing for a reason, a sign, something to give meaning to this path I'm on.

In these moments of solitude, I sit quietly with my thoughts, hoping that one day the universe will offer me a glimpse into its purpose. Until then, I live within this uncertainty, carrying these questions like a silent weight, waiting for answers that may never come.

The Solitude of Grief

Grief is a deeply personal journey, one that even those closest to us often struggle to understand. There are moments when the sadness wells up unexpectedly, like a wave crashing in the middle of an otherwise calm day. Even those who love us, who have shared our lives, cannot fully grasp why we find ourselves suddenly crying at noon or awake in the darkness, lost in memories.

Each of us carries grief in our own way, finding different means to cope. But for a mother who has lost her child, moving on is not a simple matter. It's not just something I can "bounce back" from, nor is peace something I can find by following a well-lit path. The world around me seems to expect me to heal quickly, to emerge from this sorrow as though it's merely a passing storm. But grief, I have learned, is more than just an emotion—it's an indelible mark left on the soul.

Sometimes, I feel as if the world is urging me to "move on," to "get better," as though healing is a race I must complete. There are a few compassionate hearts who allow me the space to grieve, to feel every raw emotion, to let the sadness flow as it needs to, without expectations or timelines. These are the people who understand that true healing comes in waves, in moments, in my own time.

But there are other times, other voices. One day, I heard someone very close to me—someone who, like me, is also suffering—say words that cut deeper than any wound: "What's your problem? Why are you still like this?" Their question hung in the air, a reminder of how alone one can feel, even in the company of others who share the same loss. Grief does not look the same for everyone, and yet the world often seems to expect it to.

I no longer expect others to understand the depth of my sorrow. It is a journey I walk alone, and I don't need everyone to see each step. But what would mean everything, what I long for, is simply the freedom to grieve without judgment. Just to be allowed this pain, without expectation, without pressure—that alone would be a gift.

In Every Thought, In Every Memory: Amma's Words to Nila

The Universe's Surprise

This universe gave you to me as a surprise, my little miracle, arriving just when I least expected it. But then, as quickly as you came into my life, the universe took you away, leaving me in a silence that feels endless. I find myself sitting here, night after night, surrounded by memories of you, clinging to glimpses that drift through my mind like shadows.

It's been a month without you, Nila, a month filled with an emptiness that words cannot capture. I am still here, stuck in the corner of our bed, feeling the hollow space where you should be, imagining you beside me, as if my thoughts alone could bring you back.

My dear Nila, Amma is lost without you. I don't know how to move forward or even how to live without you by my side. Every day feels like I'm learning to breathe again in a world where you are no longer here. My mind tells me to return to life, to find a routine, but my heart resists, clinging to the hope that this is all a dream, and you'll come back to me.

Wherever you are, I hope you can see me, feel the love I'm sending to you. I hope you are watching over me from somewhere, as I whisper to the universe in quiet moments, wishing you could know just how deeply I miss you. I need you to know this one thing—Amma misses you more than words can say. I miss you with every beat of my heart, and I love you with a love that will never fade.

Amma feels anger, too—anger at the universe for taking you away, for leaving me with this ache that won't go away. I hate that the same world that brought me such joy by giving me you could also be so cruel to take you from me.

Please, come back, my little Pattu... Just be back. In this silence, I wait for you, holding on to the hope that somehow, someway, you will return to me.

My dear ray of hope...

I remember the day I first knew you were coming to us, a day that felt like the beginning of a new world. Amma and Appa cried that day—tears of pure happiness and gratitude for the miracle that was you. It felt like every dream, every unspoken wish, had finally come true with the promise of you.

And then, just as suddenly as you came, you left us, leaving behind those same tears, now filled with sorrow. I hold onto the belief that, wherever you are, you are happy, that you are surrounded by love and peace, and that you carry with you the hope that you brought to us. It comforts me to think that maybe you're still out there, spreading light, just as you did for us.

Amma struggles to find the right words, the right way to express what losing you feels like. I find myself falling silent, lost in a sea of memories and dreams that are now out of reach. I often listen to a song, "Vaazhum Thodangum Idam Nee Thane"—the words echo in my heart, and every note reminds me of you. You were the beginning of our lives' greatest joy, and now, with you gone, there is a void that nothing else can fill.

I named you Nila, my celestial one, because like the moon, you appeared, bringing light and beauty, only to disappear into the vastness beyond. It's as if you were a piece of the night sky, a heavenly presence that could never fully belong to this world. I think that's why you slipped away, leaving us with only the memory of your gentle light. Wherever you are, my love, please remember that Amma misses you deeply and loves you beyond words.

Amma just misses you so much, my dear Pattu.

Raindrops and Clouds

When I look up at the clouds, I can almost feel you watching me, like a gentle presence beyond what my eyes can see. Each raindrop that falls from the sky seems like a message from you, a whisper of love sent from wherever you are.

How are you, my Pattu? Is everything okay? Amma feels like you're out there somewhere, thinking of us. I tell myself that maybe you're sending your love down to us through these raindrops, like little gifts from the heavens. All these nights without you feel so heavy, as if the weight of your absence presses down on my heart. Each day, each moment, I find myself missing you more deeply than I thought was possible.

The clouds drift by, and the rain comes and goes, but they pass through my life without you here to share them. Do you miss Amma too? I wonder if, wherever you are, you can still feel the love I have for you. I hope you're happy, wrapped in warmth and light, and that sometimes you remember us, even if only for a fleeting moment.

Whenever I stand on the balcony and watch the raindrops falling, I think of you. I remember the way you used to gaze at the rain, eyes wide with wonder, as if each drop held a tiny miracle. Now, there is rain, but you are not here to feel it with me, and that emptiness fills every corner of my heart.

Even though you're not here, my love for you remains as strong as ever. The rain brings memories, and with each one, my heart aches a little more, wishing that you could somehow return.

Love you always, my dear Pattu.

I see you in the sky,
I see you on the moon,
I see you in the stars,
I see you in the plants.

I see you in the butterflies,
I see you in the light,
I see you in the flowers,
I see you everywhere.

I feel you everywhere,
You, my guardian angel.

Hug me all you want,
Kiss me all you want,
Be with me all you want.

My little rose,
My little star,
My little joy—
I love you forever.

My dear Pattu,

People say that life goes on, that there is always something after every loss, a way to continue moving forward. But there are some losses that leave an emptiness nothing can ever fill, and losing you is one of those. Some losses are simply irreplaceable, and you, my precious one, are irreplaceable in every sense of the word.

Every day, I find myself yearning to feel your presence, to catch a hint of your scent in the air. I close my eyes, hoping that somehow, I might sense you nearby. Day by day, it gets harder, my dear Pattu. My eyes are tired from searching, and my heart aches from carrying this sorrow.

Sometimes, it feels as if you are here, a gentle presence woven into the fabric of my life. No other child ever hugged me and called me "Amma" the way you did. You were the one who held me with such love, filling my world with joy. Just the other day, I was in a restaurant and saw a child who looked a bit like you. He hugged his mother, and for a moment, I could almost feel your arms around me again.

Wherever I go, there are little reminders of you—small moments that bring you back to me, if only in memory. When I hear a child's voice calling out for their mother, when I see a little one running with arms open, I feel your presence. It's as if you're reaching out to me, letting me know you're still here, even if I can't see you.

Amma feels you, my darling. I feel your presence, and somehow, even though you're not here, I feel your touch. And yet, no matter how close I feel to you, the longing to hold you again is a constant ache.

Amma misses you every day, and my love for you will never fade. I carry you with me, always.

Amma loves you, Pattu.

Where there is light,

I hope you are there...

Where there is air,

I hope you are there...

Where there is love,

I hope you are there...

Where there is peace,

I hope you are there...

Where there is happiness,

I hope you are there...

Where there is warmth,

I hope you are there...

Where there is hope,

I see you are there...

Just let me feel the warmth,

Just let me feel the love,

Just let me feel the kindness,

Just let me feel the breath,

Just let me feel the motherhood.

Be there, my girl,

Be there, my love,

Be there, my smile,

Be there, my light.

- Amma's Chikudu

Hi, my dear Pattu,

You were my little ray of hope, a soft flicker of light that filled the darkest corners of my heart. Sometimes I wonder how I'm meant to move forward, now that you're gone. You appeared in my life like magic, your laughter like a melody I never knew I needed, and in those brief moments, you were my gift, my precious miracle.

"Why me?" I find myself asking over and over. Why was I given such a beautiful gift, only to have it taken away so soon? I loved you with every part of me, every breath, every heartbeat. Amma doesn't know if it's possible to love anyone as deeply as I loved you, my little miracle, my piece of heaven.

Since you left, sleep no longer finds me. Every night, memories of you visit me like a gentle ghost, keeping me awake as I relive the moments we shared. I search for you in the shadows, in the quiet, in everything and everywhere, as if somehow you're still just within reach.

Do you miss Amma too, my darling? I wonder if you feel this ache, this quiet, endless longing. I question if love could ever hold the same depth, the same intensity, for anyone else. You were, and will always be, my Pattu, my little miracle born from light.

Sometimes, the pain feels so deep that I wonder if it's me who has left, as if part of my soul has departed alongside you. There's an emptiness that only you can fill, a silence that only you can break. I miss you beyond words, my dear Pattu, more deeply than even my heart can understand.

Amma's heart aches for you, always.

Chella Nila,

As your Amma, I always knew you would be unique, that you would leave a mark on the world in ways that only you could. I believed you would be full of surprises, destined for a life that would shine brightly, no matter where it led you. And you proved that to me in just five short months. In every moment, you showed me a spirit so full of light, so filled with wonder.

Even in your last days, you were extraordinary. You were special in ways that words can't capture, a little angel who filled my heart with pride and my soul with love. My dear little one, I tried my best to protect you, to keep you safe, to shield you from anything that could harm you. I loved you with everything I had, and that love remains—stronger than ever. I will carry it with me until my last breath.

There are moments when I replay everything in my mind, thinking about how fragile life is, and how you, my precious Nila, were entrusted to my care. I think of how, despite all my efforts, I couldn't protect you as I should have. I feel the weight of that, the ache of wishing I could have done more, been more. I wanted so much to hold you in my arms and keep you safe from every hardship, to wrap you in a cocoon of love where nothing could touch you.

Forgive me, my Pattu. I am sorry, more than words can say. I feel the depth of that sorrow every day, knowing that you're not here, knowing that I couldn't keep you with me. Amma loves you with every beat of my heart, and I will carry this love and this ache for as long as I live.

I love you, my sweet angel. Forever and beyond.

Hello, my dear Pattu,

Today should be a happy day, a day of celebration, a day I once dreamed of sharing with you. Amma had so many plans for days like this. I imagined every little detail of how we would celebrate together, how you would light up the room with your smile, how you would be the center of all joy. But here I am, surrounded by light and laughter, and yet my heart feels hollow, for you, my life's light, are not here to share it with me.

It feels as though I am not destined for the happiness I had envisioned with you. There are lights all around me, but none of them can reach the shadows left by your absence. I find myself unable to truly feel joy, for every festive moment is a painful reminder that you're not here to be a part of it. I miss you, my sweet Pattu, with a longing so deep that I don't know if I can ever return to who I was before.

I don't know how to get back to life, how to find a "normal" when each day is marked by your absence. No day can feel complete, no celebration can feel real, without you by my side. Everywhere I turn, all I can do is think of you, to imagine how it would be if you were here, to wish for just one more moment with you.

All these celebrations around me feel empty—they remind me of a life without you, of the joy that will always feel incomplete. I miss you so much, my precious Pattu. You are in my thoughts, in my every breath, in the spaces that no one else can fill.

வானவேடிக்கைகளும்
மத்தாப்புகளும்
சிறிதும் நிகரில்லையடி
என் நிலாவின் முகஒளிக்கு

(Even the fireworks and all the smiles cannot compare to the light of my moon's face.)

Hello, my sweet Pattu,

How are you, my precious Chikkudu? Amma's thoughts are always wrapped around you, holding onto every memory, every moment. Wherever I go, whatever I see, it feels as if the world is gently offering me glimpses of you, as if everything carries a piece of you within it. I miss you more than words can convey. I miss the warmth of your little hands, the way your smile lit up every corner of my heart, the sparkle in your eyes that could brighten even the darkest days.

There are moments when a familiar scent drifts by—jasmines in bloom—and suddenly, I'm surrounded by memories of you. It's as if each jasmine petal carries a piece of your presence, bringing you closer, if only for a fleeting instant. These flashes of you are like precious photographs etched into my heart, each memory vivid, beautiful, and cherished. It's almost as if they are fragments of time that keep you with me, allowing me to feel you even when you're so far away.

I find myself longing for you in every quiet moment, searching for the familiar comfort of your presence. I cling to the hope that you are in a beautiful place now, somewhere filled with love and peace, where happiness surrounds you as it once surrounded me when you were here. Sometimes, a wave of guilt washes over me, for crying, for feeling this emptiness so deeply. I worry, wondering if my little Pattu would want to see Amma this way. But I am only human, my dear, and this separation weighs so heavily on my heart.

For those five precious months, I never left your side—not even for a moment. We were inseparable, my love, bound together in a world that felt complete and whole. Now, life has put this vast distance between us, and I find myself searching for you in everything beautiful. I hope you are happy somewhere, watching the skies, playing among the birds and butterflies, and basking in all that is pure and gentle. Every time I look at the moon, I feel as if you are gazing back at me, your light reaching me even across this distance.

You are my moon, my star, my eternal light, watching over me, guiding me. Love you forever, my precious Pattu.

The Scripted Journey

All my life, I've been told that everything happens for a reason. It's a phrase that has echoed since my childhood, a reassurance offered to soothe life's unexpected turns. But now, I find myself asking, "What exactly is the reason?" Why must a living soul endure so much suffering, only to eventually fade from this world, leaving behind those who loved them?

What is the purpose of this journey, this endless cycle of joy and pain? Why must one's heart be broken, only to continue on, bearing the weight of loss? If life is indeed a carefully written script, why does it feel so heavy, so difficult to comprehend?

Nila, you taught me something invaluable, even in your short time here. You showed me the importance of spreading happiness, of making the most of each moment, however fleeting. Your life reminded me that every smile, every shared joy, is a treasure. But, you also left me with a profound lesson—one that I still struggle to accept. In this world, we can't hold onto those we love forever. No matter how deeply we wish, we cannot ask someone to stay beyond their time, nor can we stop them from leaving.

Life, it seems, is a story already written, and we are merely actors, moving along a path we didn't choose. We're playing our roles, following a script whose ending we cannot see. And while this thought brings a sense of helplessness, I hold on to the hope that you, my sweet Nila, are still close to us in spirit.

I feel your presence around me, like a quiet strength that keeps me moving forward. I hope, wherever you are, that you're proud of us—of our attempts to live on, to carry on with the pieces we have left. I am doing my best to be strong, to honor the love we shared, and to live a life you would smile upon.

I miss you, Nila, every moment of every day. You are forever in my heart.

No Reverse Button

Hi, my dear Pattu,

Sometimes, I wish life had a reverse button. A single press to undo the unbearable moments, to rewrite the days that have left me aching. But reality settles in, and I am reminded that there is no such button, no magic way to turn back time. All I can do is count the days that pass, trying my best to move forward, even though each step feels like lifting a mountain.

"There is always a life after every loss," they say. It's a phrase I hear often, words meant to comfort, but they echo hollowly. People around me tell me to keep going, to find hope in the future, but it's not that simple. Some days, even the thought of getting out of bed, of just existing, feels like an impossible task. The smallest of tasks—chores, routines—seem to pull at every bit of energy I have, draining me.

There are times when the weight of grief feels too heavy to carry in public, times when I want to break down but hold back because I don't want to hear the same familiar reassurances, the same well-meaning but empty words. I don't want to have the same conversations that remind me of what's gone, and yet, I can't bear to be alone with the negative thoughts that fill my mind.

I don't know how many people understand the heaviness that fills the heart, the way each breath feels like a struggle, as though I am carrying an invisible weight that presses down on my chest. It's a burden that's hard to describe—a sorrow so deep that it feels physical, something that makes even the act of breathing feel laborious.

You know, Pattu, Amma just feels... heavy-hearted.

Life After Loss

I often find myself wondering what it truly means to live in a world where someone you love so deeply is no longer by your side. There were moments when I believed that such a time would never come, that loss was a distant shadow I would never have to face. And yet, here I am, living in a world that feels both familiar and foreign, navigating a reality reshaped by your absence.

This journey feels strange, like I'm learning to walk in darkness with only the faint glow of your memory to guide me. Sometimes, all I have are fleeting glimpses of you—flashes that visit me unexpectedly, as if your spirit is dancing just beyond my reach. In the quiet moments, or even amidst a crowd, I can feel you there, a gentle presence reminding me of what we shared. And in those moments, the ache of missing you is both a comfort and a pain, an unshakable part of me.

Grief is unlike any other challenge I've faced. I've endured hardship before, but this... this is a new kind of struggle, a raw and relentless sorrow that lives within me. I close my eyes, and all I see is your face, as clear as if you were right here. I find myself yearning for the smallest details—your scent, your laugh, the warmth of your smile. It feels like I am reaching for something just beyond my grasp, something I will never again hold.

Sometimes, in those fleeting moments, it almost feels as if you are here with me, as if you're standing beside me, just as you once did. And then, like a wave crashing, reality returns, and I am left standing in the empty silence, realizing that you are gone. It's as if my life has become frozen in time, each day trapped in the shadow of September 5th, the last day I knew true happiness. That day marks the dividing line between before and after, the day you took all of my joy with you.

Now, I find myself here, pen in hand, trying to pour out these feelings, to make sense of a world that has lost its color without you. I write to you, hoping that, somewhere, you are reading these words, feeling each unspoken emotion, understanding the depths of love and loss woven into every letter.

Sometimes, it feels like I am writing into the void, but I imagine you, my little one, on the other side, reading and understanding, as if these words are our connection across time and space.

Nila: "Verses from the Heart"

> *"In words and in silence, your memory remains
> an eternal melody within my heart."*

In these lines, I find a language that transcends time—a way to speak to my Nila in words that reflect the depth of my love. Each verse is a part of me, a whisper of my soul, a reminder that love endures beyond the boundaries of life. Here, in the language of my heart, I leave a part of myself for you, my precious Nila

நிலாவுடன் நான்

ஒரு இரவில் உதித்த நீ
ஒரு நொடியில் மறைந்த நீ
ஒரு யுகமாயினும் மறவா நீ

என் நிலா

காணாத மேகமும்
மழைத்துளியும்
மண் வாசனையும்
நீண்ட இரவும்
கடிக்கர ஒலியும்
நாள்காட்டி அசைவும்
காக்கை கூச்சலும்
மாடியின் படியும்
நீர்விட்ட மூங்கிலும்
படுக்கையின் ஓரமும்
சுமந்த என் கண்களும்
தேடுதடி உன்னை

என் நிலா

வெள்ளை மேகங்களும்
பச்சை இலைகளும்
நிறமில்லா மழைத்துளிகளும்
கருந்த இரவுகளும்
நீலக் கடல்களும்
சிவந்த சூரியனிலும் கூட
அம்மா காண்பது கண்மணி,

உன்னையே என் நிலா

தெரிந்தோ தெரியாமலோ அம்மா உன்னை
நிலவாக்கினேன்
இன்றும் அந்த வானத்தில் காண்கிறேன்
தேய்ந்துகொண்டும் இருக்கிறாய்
வளர்ந்துகொண்டும் இருக்கிறாய்
அந்த வானத்தில்
அம்மாவும் நம்புகிறேன்
ஒரு நாள் வருவாய்
என்னிடம் முழுநிலவாக

இரவின் நீளமும்
பகலின் பாரமும்
கண்ணில் ஈரமும்
இதயத்தின் கனமும்
உந்தன் நினைவும்
சிறிதும் குறையவில்லையடி
என் நிலவே

நான்கு திசையும்
மூன்று வேலையும்
இரண்டு உயிரும்
ஒரு நொடி மறவாமல்
உன்னை நினைத்து என் நிலவே

இதயம் துடிப்பதும் ஒரு வலி ஆகுதடி
உன் மறைவினில்
என் நிலவே

மண்ணில் உயிரை ஈன்ற போதும்
தடுமாறி கீழே விழுந்த போதும்
தயங்கி தயங்கி நடந்த போதும்
ஓடி ஆடி நின்ற போதும்
விழித்து படித்து பயின்ற போதும்
உழைத்து பிழைத்து வாழ்ந்த போதும்
கண்டு வியந்து கட்டிய போதும்
கட்டி பிடுத்து கலந்த போதும்
கையில் தன்னுயிர் வந்த போதும்
தன்னுயிர் தன்னை கடிந்த போதும்
இறுதியில் மண்ணுக்குள் சென்ற போதும்
எஞ்சியது என்றும் வலியே ஆகும்

In the silence left behind, I have found fragments of love and resilience that only Nila could have gifted me. Her light, though brief, now fills every corner of my heart. Through her, I've come to understand that some bonds transcend the physical, woven instead into the fabric of the soul. This journey, colored by both the beauty of her presence and the ache of her absence, has reshaped me, leaving me with memories as deep as the ocean and a love as boundless as the sky. Nila, you are forever woven into the essence of who I am.

A Heart's Offering: Words from a lost soul

I dedicate this to all those who find it difficult to move forward—you are not alone. I am here with you, another lost soul still seeking a way to reclaim life. This journey, as painful as it may be, is beyond what any of us can control. My psychologist once told me that birth, death, and all that happens in between are beyond our grasp; we cannot alter what unfolds. Instead, we must live in the flow of life and allow ourselves to adapt, however slowly. Taking extreme steps is not a solution—it's merely an escape from life itself.

There is a phrase in Tamil: Sogathil perum sogam puthira sogam (the deepest sorrow is the loss of a child). There are people around us who find a way to carry on, even in the face of such unimaginable loss. So why can't we all move forward, despite our own struggles? No loss is small; every loss leaves its own wound. Grieve as much as you need, and carry the memories with you. They will travel alongside you, a quiet presence in each step forward.

I am here, too, trying to make sense of what life can still offer, still questioning, still searching. And so, the journey continues.

In the Quiet of Your Soul

*"In the quiet spaces of our hearts, we find the
words that we didn't know we carried. Let this be
a place for those whispered truths to be heard."*